Pirates

JC Alva

Published by JC Alva, 2023.

PIRATES

First edition. January 26, 2023.

Copyright © 2023 JC Alva.

ISBN: 979-8215661611

Written by JC Alva.

To my wife Rosanna and my children,

Marielle and Josh, Luis, and Rio.

May happiness always be always your companion in life.

Love Dad.

Pirates
By JC Alva

Sitting on the co-pilot's chair of the cargo carrier ship is Cheryl Thompson, a young trainee who had, just seven months ago, graduated from an off-world academy and has been assigned to the Titan 3, a large interplanetary cargo vessel that transports resources from uninhabited planets for different colonies.

The fair-skinned; black-haired beauty had her eyes trained on several monitors reflecting off her front forward window. Her blue eyes constantly move from one monitor to the next while trying to assist the docking of a smaller craft that shuttles materials from the planet below to the Titan 3 in stationary orbit.

"Shuttle 235, please proceed to dock 14,"
Cheryl says in a stern commanding voice.
"Roger that. Proceeding to dock 14"
The shuttle pilot responds.
"Shuttle 235, Please decrease your approach speed and follow the systems tracking waypoint, Copy?"

She squints and lowers her eyebrows as she is visibly annoyed by the shuttle's approach. Then suddenly, A voice from behind her says
"Having trouble with 235 again?"

The captain of the ship, grey-haired with a constant stern look on his face, walks briskly into the bridge.

"Sir! No sir, just part of the job sir!"

Cheryl answers just the way she was taught at the academy.

"Relax First Officer Trainee Thompson."

As the captain takes his seat on the bridge, he starts tapping his glass-surfaced keyboard and then reads the ship's general status.

"What's our current load capacity?"

Cheryl switches her monitors.

"About 72 percent sir. We will be hitting 80% when shuttle 235 completes his load."

The captain gestures at another crew member to get his usual cup of coffee.

"Then we must be ahead of schedule, First Officer Thompson. Your calculations for our new orbital position have helped accelerate our shuttle's return from their extraction point."

The captain breaks a small smile at the corner of his lips, almost hiding his satisfaction for Thompson's work from the rest of the crew.

"Thank you, sir. Just doing my job sir, as I was taught at the academy."

Cheryl answers while not even breaking her eyes from her monitors. She compiles a summary of all her loading schedules during her shift and then returns the monitor to regular tracking.

The other crew member returns to the captain with his coffee.

He graciously thanks the crew member and turns to Cheryl with a hot cup of coffee on his lips. He quietly looks at her entries and notices her deleting the last tracking record of the last ship entering the Titan.

The captain turns his attention back to his forward monitors and checks the ship's overall status.

"First Officer Akita will now take the Trainees' seat. You're training so far has been going very well, let's not push it. Time for you to get a little rest."

"Yes Sir, thank you, sir."

"First Officer Akita now has the chair."

Cheryl unbuckles her seat harness, pushes her control monitors to the side, stands up, pulls her uniform down to remove the creases on her shoulders, and faces the captain, giving a quick, sharp salute.

The captain responds with a snappy salute. She turns around and walks towards a cylindrical lift, taking off her officer's cap and placing it under her right armpit.

She starts walking to the rear of the bridge where the other trainees and regular officers were stationed.

Before reaching the lift, one of the lady officers whispers to her...

"Psst!... Are you meeting Robert at the bar?"

She smiles and looks back at the captain to see if he noticed them talking.

She sees the captain busy with some planetary charts with First Officer Akita scanning the different sectors where they have been extracting metal deposits on the planet.

"What's it to you?"

The lady officer smiles at Cheryl and hands her some credits. She looks back again at the captain and then says:

"What's this for?"

"Can you forward this to the Bartender? I was supposed to pay that last night but got too drunk to do so..."

Cheryl looks at the credits already in her hand.

"This looks like a lot! Did you throw a party last night at the bar?"

The lady officer blushes...

"I treated Michael last night..."

Cheryl gives her a disgusted smile and says

"You mean you treated Michael's whole group of friends last night"

"But it was his birthday..."

Cheryl walks closer to the lady officer.

"You know that Michael does this to all his girlfriends. You don't have to keep on doing this. You should leave his free-loading ass behind! You can do better."

The lady officer takes back her credits and turns away from Cheryl.

The door of the lift chimes, and Cheryl puts her hand lightly on the woman's shoulder.

She keeps her eyes on her monitors not wanting to hear what Cheryl has to say.

"I mean it! You're a very pretty officer with a promising career. Don't mess it all up for someone who can't even have his own cabin at his age. He will just suck you dry till there is nothing left. And I'm not talking about money dear..."

She presses the glass sensors and the lift's doors slide open. She enters the lift and turns around.

Just before the lift doors close, Cheryl sees the lady officer looking at the credits in her hand then looks at Cheryl.

Her lips say "Thank you." Silently, just before the sliding door closes.

Cheryl presses the feather light buttons of the lift that brings her to the recreation area. She smiles knowing that she has, in her own little way, encouraged another woman to break her emotional chains.

A light chime sounded then the lift doors opened to a corridor on the recreational level.

She walks past small convenience stores and cafés that were already occupied by other cadets and engineers.

She would wave her hand, nod, and smile occasionally when she sees some of her fellow cadet trainees with regular ship crews along the way.

She sees Michael with some of his buddies in a French Café. She sees him sitting down beside another new lady trainee. His arm was around the backrest of her French café seat, sweet talking his way into her cabin and into her credits.

Cheryl reaches the entrance to the ship's bar and places her right-hand band on a sensor beside the bar entrance. Her name and rank flash on an amber panel and the door slides open.

The lights were soft dim blue, walls covered by reproduction ancient pictures of great jazz musicians that were lit by tiny spotlights on the ceilings. There were classic small lamps in the center of each round table and soft jazz music was playing while holograms of ancient musical artists were projected on the stage.

She walks towards the bar made of artificial green Italian marble and its edges made of rosewood with intricate ancient Earth 1930s reproduction carvings.

Cheryl sits on a bar stool and calls the metallic robot bartender.

"Hello, Johnny!

The Robot had a Human-like metallic face and hands and was dressed like an old western bartender wearing a vest and tie, and rubber laces on each upper arm. It moves in through a rail behind the bar and quickly stopped in front of Cheryl.

"Good evening, Miss Cheryl, wonderful night for music isn't it?"

"Yes, it is Johnny."

"What may I ask would be your preferred drink for tonight?"

"How about…A dry martini this time."

"Superb choice Miss Cheryl. We just got a fresh batch of olives delivered yesterday from Martian Farms. They say it's the most genetically perfect olives in the system."

"Oh yes! I remembered assisting them in docking yesterday…"

"Would you like something to eat to go with your martini Miss Cheryl?"

"How about a plate of Spanish Cold cuts with cheese…"

"That would be my choice as well Miss Cheryl"

The Robot excuses himself as he turns around and reaches for his ingredients to make the martini.

The bar was starting to fill with other crew members getting off their duties, and the sound from the holograms was slowly being drowned out by some laughter and inaudible conversations.

The robot serves her a martini.

"Oh Johnny, before I forget, Officer Jennie says that last night's expenses are to be charged to Michael Beck's Account since he and his friends were the ones who consumed the food and drinks, his birthday, they say."

"Yes Miss Cheryl, as it was obvious to all…"

The Robot bartender Johnny momentarily freezes and his artificial eyes blink red, then green.

"Miss Cheryl, I have now cleared Officer Jennie's account of last night's expenses and have transferred it to Michael Becks's Account."

"Thank you, Johnny. Can you also inform Officer Jennie through her personal communicator when you see Michael Beck here in the bar?"

"My system has access to all communicators, but since I have already transferred the debts to Mr. Michael Beck's account, his accumulated unpaid credits will automatically keep him from entering this establishment till he settles his credit debts in the main collection office."

Cheryl smiles at Johnny and lifts her martini to him.

"Thank you, Johnny."

"Glad to be of Service."

She looks at herself in the mirror, between the bottles of wines and spirits on the Bar's shelves in front of her lifting her glass as she cheers herself on completing another day's work at the bridge as a cadet trainee.

She picks up the toothpick that had a green olive off her glass and took the olive between her front red lips, sipping its juices before finally chewing the whole olive in her mouth.

"Mmm! Love those Martian Olives!"

She then reaches into one of her pockets and brings out a smooth, shiny, flat, circular green stone.

A sweet manly voice came from behind her

"Hey... Cheryl! You still got that good luck charm of yours, eh?"

"Robert! You done with your unloading already?"
Cheryl felt awakened by his presence.
"You know me, I work fast"
He says while trying to give Cheryl a quick kiss. She quickly puts up the green stone to block his lips from hers.
"Not so fast! You did It again?"
"Did what?" he asks, grabbing her hand and twisting it around her waist.
Cheryl snaps. "You purposely went out of line again on your approach! You know how much hate that!"
"C'mon Honey... You know I love you..."
Says Robert. Cheryl takes another sip of her martini.
"The captain is beginning to notice your sloppy approach. It's a good thing I got to erase your approach record on the system without the captain noticing."
Robert lets go of Cheryl and then sits down beside her on the bar. He calls the robot bartender.
"Hello, Johnny! How's it hanging?"

"My parts still seem to be intact Sir Robert...May I take your order, sir?"

Robert starts laughing at the robot's answer and orders a beer. He removes a satchel bag hanging from across his chest and lays it on the bar. He opens up the satchel bag and starts reaching for items inside the bag.
"I see you still have time for your hobby ..."
Cheryl says as she takes another sip from her drink.
Robert opens the satchel and brings out two small items. One item was a tiny elongated insect-like droid with

sharp-clawed appendages that moved in a multi-directional manner and its tiny remote control.

Robert lays the droid on the marble bar top and pushes a switch on the droid's head. Its tiny LCD eyes lit up and it started powering itself to its feet.

"Robert, Stop it! I'm not gonna be helping you pay for the damages that droid toy of yours will do..."

"Relax..." says Robert, as he takes out his tiny remote control and presses a button.

The droid starts making whirling sounds and starts analyzing its surroundings.

"O.K, Robert, that doesn't sound right..."

"What do you mean doesn't sound right?"

The droid suddenly dashes away from them going down the bar and hitting glasses, pitchers of other customers. It causes everyone at the bar to stand up and grab their drinks to keep themselves from being splashed by the out-of-control droid.

Johnny the bartender rushes his way to grab the droid off the bar just before he could reach a set of expensive bottles of Japanese scotch whiskey at the end of the bar.

Its claws start scratching the robot's metal hands while Robert rushes to the bars end and turns off the droid. Robert, while holding his droid walks back to Cheryl's seat while he apologizes to the bothered customers.

Cheryl smiles at Robert and says...

"You were saying..."

Robert, fidgeting on his droid

"I've been studying up on the uses of tiny droids. Turns out, the military limits our onboard files on droids with regards to its other uses; for covert ops, sabotage, that kind of stuff. I actually, had to ask a friend to lend me his access code to get more information about these things..."

Cheryl takes another sip of her martini.

"I Guess all boys need their toys..."

"Toys?! These are not Toys!"

"Who are you kidding?"

Johnny the Bartender comes back to Cheryl and Robert.

"I hope my damage is not big this time?"

Johnny the Bartender smiles at Robert

"You're in luck, Sir Robert! A memo came in today regarding the coverage of our insurance. It turns out our new policy includes damages caused by Mechanical Systems, Robots, Yours truly and droids."

"This must be my lucky day!"

"It seems like it Sir. All the drinks spilled are all courtesy of our Corporate legal team."

Robert raises his glass of beer and says

"Here's to our Corporate lawyers! Cheers!"

As the other customers at the bar get their fresh drink replacements, they look at Robert and raise their glasses.

Robert Smiles back at them while raising his glass.

Cheryl looks at Robert and puts her arm around his waist.

"You really want to talk about your toy hobby or would you rather we just get out of here?"

Robert grabs his droid off the bar and returns it into his satchel. He slings the satchel across his chest and leaves Johnny with a credit tip.

Cheryl bottoms up her glass and leaps out of her bar stool. Robert grabs her by the waist and makes their way toward the exit.

The sliding door opens and they see Michael Beck trying to scan his wrist ID on the entrance door, which keeps beeping back a red "No Entry" sign, which usually means pay up or stay out. Cheryl sees the young trainee embarrassed by the Non-entry status. The young trainee turns to her friends

"Hey guys, let's just go to the Bora Club, at least my ID will accept us there."

Michael Beck's ears turn blood red in embarrassment and is left standing by himself at the bar's entrance, having to give way to others waiting in line to enter.

"Payback's a Bitch!"

"What's that?" Asked Robert.

Cheryl smiles and says "Oh...Nothing!"

A few hours later, the ship's Captain was on the bridge sending a recording to his family. First Officer Akita was monitoring the last few shuttles flying in their mineral loads into the Titan when the navigation officer noticed the scanners have picked up a new signal.

"Sir, there is an unidentified vessel approaching..."

The captain turns off his message recorder and says,

"On my monitor please"

First Officer Akita looks at her monitors.

"That ship is not one of ours, nor does it have any commercial configuration of the ships we trade with sir."

The captain quickly studies the scans.

"Nav Officer, sound alert level two and contact IC. First officer Akita, please deliver the standard message to that ship. Try to find out who they are. How long before Interplanetary Command gets here?"

"About Five hours sir," Akita replied.

The captain checks his instruments and makes a quick calculation of the unidentified ship's speed.

"At their present speed, they could board us in less than thirty minutes."

First Officer Akita tries to make contact with the approaching ship.

"This is CCS Titan 3 calling on approaching ship, you are in restricted orbital space, and therefore unauthorized to be within this commercial zone. Please identify yourself or we will contact the Interplanetary Command to apprehend your vessel."

While the message was being transmitted, another officer noticed an interference.

"Sir, they seem to be jamming our signal to the IC."

The captain looks at his monitor and then turns to the first officer.

"Put the ship on the main Screen please..."

First officer Akita passes her fingers on her control panel and makes some entries. Another officer on the bridge suddenly says.

"Sir, our sensors pick up the activation of their weapons systems, and they have activated their forward shields."

First officer Akita confirms the reading and turns to the captain.

"Captain, the ship is now on the main screen..."

The wide forward window projects a large elongated black ship with its turrets coming out of its forward sections.

The black ship opens up its side compartments and three unmanned probes flew out of the black ship and started rushing toward the Titan.

"Captain, the ship is sending out probes to scan us."

The captain views the probes on his forward display and asks his officers to monitor them.

The probes swiftly fly around the huge carrier scanning its interior.

In one of the lower compartments of the Titan, an old man sitting at his work table hears a light rattle coming from inside his metal locker. He slowly stands and goes in front of his locker. He opens it and looks inside...

"They found us!"

By this time, the whole ship was placed on general alert. Cheryl and Robert were suddenly awakened by the alarm sounds and flashing lights in their quarters.

"Get up! somethings happening!"

Cheryl says as she jumps out of bed leaving Robert to slowly rise scratching his head.

"What's going on?"

"I don't know, but sure as hell, I'm not gonna be the last one to find out!"

She hurriedly jumps into her red-orange body-fit jumpsuit uniform, zips herself up, and heads toward the door.

"Get to your station! I'll see you later."

Meanwhile, at the bridge, the captain and First Officer Akita are busy attempting to send messages to different Orbital Stations.

The black ship started firing its forward guns damaging a compartment just below the bridge and sending large metal debris spinning into space.

The Titan shook with every hit as the captain was holding onto his captain's seat.

"Pirates!" says the captain, as everyone on the bridge gazed at a black vessel, about a fourth the size of their cargo ship.

"Security personnel on the defensive guns! Now!" Shouts the captain.

Officer Akita reaches for a large round button on top of her center console and slams her palm down on it.

The Titan's alarms activate throughout the ship, red flashing lights replace the regular cool blue lights of the corridors as all personnel starts rushing toward their assigned positions.

Security personnel jumps on a line of seats along the inside walls of the Titan. They strap themselves in while the chairs automatically start moving towards the lateral walls of the Titan that mechanically opens up to defensive guns with a view of the Pirate ship already beside them.

Before they could start firing back at the pirate ship, some of the guns were blasted by the lateral guns of the attacking ship. The Titan's security started firing, doing little damage as the attacking ship's outer shields were too strong to have any effect by their smaller defensive guns.

The pirate ship quickly maneuvered and stabilized its position beside the Titan and continued firing with its smaller lateral guns, destroying the defensive guns, killing the security personnel manning them, and damaging portions of the Titan's exterior walls.

The Titan takes a hit on one of its huge external thrusters which affected the internal power of the Titan.

The remaining defensive guns of the titan go offline and the security officers manning them try their best to reactivate them.

With every hit, the Titan was jolted and emergency warnings on the status panels were all flashing red.

Then, just as suddenly the attack came, the Pirate ship ceases its firing and began maneuvering closer on the right side of the Titan.

The Pirate's ship huge metal doors slide open and a large mechanical umbilical bridge started extending out of the pirate ship. Its end reaches the surface of the Titan's hull and magnetically clamped itself on the side of the Titan.

The Pirates, wearing all-black space suites had their helmets on, which had dark tinted glass that concealed their faces. They were all heavily armed with compact battle rifles and were all rearing to board the Titan.

A Pirate presses a button beside the wall and an exterior door opens to the lighted interior of the Umbilical Bridgeway attached to the Titan's surface. He leads the pirates floating down the tube followed by a large number of Pirates.

Cheryl was running toward the bridge. She sees all other personnel running in different directions toward their own assigned emergency positions.

The ship shudders and sways, she grabs a wall handle to keep herself from falling as the lights on the ship's corridors flicker.

Cheryl sees cadet trainees helping wounded security officers who have survived while manning their defensive guns.

She sees more security personnel carrying rifles running towards where the pirates had clamped on the Titan.

She started to pick up her pace going in the same direction as the security officers, when suddenly, a few meters in front of her, the wall of the corridor exploded. The blast threw her and the security officers back from where they came from, dazed and hard of hearing from the explosion.

Her ears were still ringing and could only hear muffled sounds.

While slowly trying to get up to recover, she could see two figures in black space suits climbing into the corridor from the blasted wall opening.

Her hearing started coming back when she could start hearing the security officers yelling instructions to one another while the loud sounds of gunfire erupted in the corridor.

Cheryl could also see through the white smoke some Titan security men firing off their weapons at the black-suited pirates who have now dispersed and started firing down other connecting corridors.

Cheryl remained low on the floor as a sudden firefight erupted in the corridor. Bullets bounced off the walls and the air started to smell of burning materials, as smoke started floating through the corridors.

One by one she could see the security men being shot down, till the last one standing behind a thick post gets hit and falls not far beside her. His blood started spilling toward her. The dying man's eyes were staring at her in fear as his breathing started to slow down. His rifle was about a meter away from Cheryl.

As she was about to reach for the weapon, a blast hit the ground between her extended arm and the rifle, and the two black spacemen stood over her.

"Don't even think about it!" The Pirate said through the space suit, making a barely audible sound through his helmet.

Cheryl froze.

"Get up!" the second pirate says with a distinct woman's voice.

Cheryl slowly gets up and one of the Pirates picks up the dead soldier's weapon and slings it on his shoulders.

The Pirate with the woman's voice shoved Cheryl from behind...

"Move it!"

The sound of sporadic gunfire started to die down the pirates gather the surrendering crew of the Titan.

The Titan's captain and his bridge officers sealed themselves from the attacking pirates.

Loud banging on the metal door resonated inside the bridge, scaring the younger cadet trainees whose faces were now filled with fear.

"They will soon breach those doors. Just follow their instructions. Pirates usually just come for the cargo, not the crew. Whatever happens, Stay alive!"

The Banging stopped and for a few seconds, silence.

The metal door exploded inwards as the crew covered themselves behind their consoles. Pirates moved in with their weapons pointing at the crew.

"Who is the captain?!"

The Titan crew were rounded up and brought to the loading dock level, the biggest part of the ship with an open area where they could easily monitor all their prisoners.

They separated the rest of the crew from the security personnel, and herded them down to the cargo hold, locking them in large metal storage containers.

"Where's the captain and First Officer?"

Cheryl whispered to the cadet beside her.

"Some saw him being brought to the rec level with their leader"

The Cadet answers. Then Cheryl whispers to the cadet

"But why are they busy rounding us up? Pirates usually just take the cargo and leave. They know that the IC is on their way and they can't risk that..."

Cheryl started looking around for Robert. She started feeling sorry for leaving him in her quarters when the alarms went off.

"I hope he is safe," she said to herself.

Two Pirates, with their space helmets removed, were patrolling making sure there were no remaining crew members of the commercial vessel loose in the ship.

As they were walking around the main power silo compartment of the ship, they had to go single file on a slim catwalk just above the main fusion reactors.

There were different-sized cooling pipes running above the catwalks. Suddenly, from the pipes above, swung a large metal wrench that hit the second pirate on his head. The Pirate falls into the large silo screaming. Before the first pirate could react, Robert jumped down and landed on the catwalk striking the pirate's rifle off his hands with the large mechanical wrench.

The Pirate lunged at Robert and sent him to the catwalk floor. The Pirate pulled out a secondary weapon off his belt, but before he could use it, Robert, kicked the pirate's knee and sent him tumbling down the fusion bay silo.

The echoing sound of the pirate's scream and the clanging sound of his suit hitting the walls and bottom of the fusion reactor was deafening.

Soon the echoes faded into silence, with the faint humming sound of the fusion reactors below him. As Robert was getting on his feet, he turned around to see the rifle of the first pirate he attacked was still lying on the catwalk. He grabs the rifle, slings it on his shoulder, and starts heading toward the upper levels of the ship.

Cheryl was lined up with the rest of the trainees, while the regular crew was corralled in another group. They were sitting on the floor with their hands tied behind their backs, with two pirates standing on both ends of each group.

A woman pirate came to the cadets and started looking at each of them one by one. She had golden long hair, tied ponytailed with a bright red metallic ribbon. She had a scar that ran from the bottom of her left green eye all the way down to her upper lip.

With the same familiar voice Cheryl heard earlier, the woman pirate says,

"He wants the Officer Trainees now!"

She turns around whipping her golden hair and starts walking away. The guard points his weapon at the group.

"The four of you! Get up!"

The prisoners and Cheryl struggled to get up with their hands tied. They were led to one of the ship's lifts. When they got to the Recreation level, there were more pirates in the corridors.

Cheryl could notice some of the pirates smashing display counters with different merchandise in them while they were walking down the corridor.

Cheryl could still hear the jazz music playing as they were near the entrance of the bar. The chairs and tables were in disarray, bar stools were thrown behind the counter, where the robotic bartender stood, vandalized but still functioning.

They were brought around the bar's corner, seeing the captain tied to a chair, painfully bleeding from his nose, cheek, and mouth. In front of him, sitting on a stool, was a burly bald pirate, sweating, his bare knuckles stained with the captain's blood.

Cheryl saw First Officer Akita on another chair, tied, also battered, and bloodied. Her mouth was gagged, and she looked passed out. At her feet was Officer Jennie, whom she last saw on the bridge. Her body lay lifeless with a bullet hole in her chest.

A voice came from a dark corner of the bar.

"The captain does not want to be cooperative…"

A tall dark man with a blue mohawk haircut started walking out of the darkness. He was wearing an Exotic spotted fur coat of an animal from another colonized planet. He wore black cargo pants and boots that had several buckles running up the side.

He had large jeweled gold rings on almost every finger, thick long golden chains hanging from his neck covering his bare hairy chest. His thick cigar gave off a bad incense-like smell, as it is smoke floated up and caught the flickering colors projected by the hologram projectors.

He walks closer to the tied captain, taking a puff and flicking his ashes on the captain's head he asked,

"Where is the Relic, Captain?"

The captain slowly lifts his head and faces the blue-haired pirate.

"I really don't know what you're talking about…"

The captain takes another hit in the face from the bald pirate.

Cheryl noticed the lady pirate sitting by herself on the same bar stool she last sat on, having a beer. She glances at Cheryl, then looks away as soon as Cheryl looks at her.

The pirate captain once again takes a deep puff of his cigar and while exhaling a thick cloud of smoke, brings his cigar close to the captain's lap.

"Captain, I really don't want to stay on your ship any longer than I have to. Just give me the relic and we will be on our way...No need for further bloodshed...No?"

The captain spits blood to the floor and looks up again at the pirate.

"This is the CCS Titan 3; our mission is to extract raw minerals from assigned planets for..." Before the captain could finish, the pirate pushed the thick burning side of his cigar into the captain's thigh, burning through his uniform. The captain lets out a scream while his body shutters on the chair he was tied to.

All the Trainees looked away as their captain was being questioned.

Cheryl figured that the Dark Blue-haired Pirate was their leader.

"If this captain is willing to take much pain, and sacrifice one of his officers, then maybe he can have a little more concern for his young cadet trainees."

As soon as the pirate captain said those words, the four trainees were shoved down to kneeling positions. The captain looked at the Pirate and said

"No! Keep them out of this! I really don't know anything about a relic..."

Suddenly a shot rang out, and one of the trainees fell dead on the floor. The captain kept his eyes closed not wanting to see the dead cadet in front of him.

The burly bald man grabbed the captain's head and forced his face to the dead cadet.

"Look at your Cadet! He is dead because of you!"

The Pirate Captain brings out a torch lighter and relights his extinguished cigar. He takes quick deep puffs on his cigar till the lighter relights the glowing end of the cigar. Thick smoke bellows out of his mouth and puffs a circle of smoke in the air that is lit up by the spotlights on the bar's ceiling.

Then there was the sound of another loading gun, ready to fire at the next prisoner.

Cheryl yelled "Stop! I know where it is!"

The cadets took a large sigh of relief. The pirate leader stood up and walked towards Cheryl.

"Where is it, Child?"

As he puffs on his cigar, he reads her nametag

"Cadet Officer trainee Cheryl Thompson."

Cheryl answers "it's down below, I can take you to it."

The pirate captain points at two other pirates in the room

"Go with her and bring it to me."

The two pirates grabbed Cheryl by her arms to stand her up. She led her two captors back down the hall towards another lift.

She sees more pirates rummaging through the different stores and offices along the way, carrying stolen items in storage boxes.

She led her two guards down to the cargo area where mining equipment was locked in different large containers.

She stopped in front of a container that had an alphanumeric keyboard, which allowed entry to the container.

"I need both hands to enter the code..."

The pirate closest to Cheryl pulled out a knife and cut her restraints. She rubbed her reddened wrists and started punching in a code.

Cheryl thought to herself:

"What the hell am I doing? I don't even know what they are looking for."

The guards grew impatient. "Open it already!!!"

Cheryl finally punches in the last key. The sound of the hydraulic gates was low-toned and loud. She steps into the container followed by one of her captors, passing the light switch, where there were different-sized boxes with labels on them. Her eyes glance at a few metal pipes just resting above the boxes near the entrance of the container.

"It's somewhere back there..." Cheryl tells the pirate.

He steps sideways to make his way through the stacked boxes. Suddenly, gunshots rang out. The pirate turns around and starts heading outside to see what is happening. Cheryl grabs a metal pipe resting on the boxes and swings it at the pirate's head, knocking him out cold. She then takes and shoulders the pirate's weapon and grabs his sidearm.

A few seconds later, the shooting had stopped, and Cheryl came out of the container aiming her rifle forward. She peeks outside to see a man kneeling over the other pirate's body, searching for more items he could use.

"Robert!"

Robert gave her a smile and said, "You miss me?"

Cheryl slings her rifle across her chest to her back and gives Robert a tight hug.

"Wow! I know you miss me, but I didn't think that much..."

"I thought you were dead!"

Robert gently pulls back and continues to go through the dead pirate's body.

"So why are they still here? Isn't it unusual for pirates to linger in a ship like this?"

Cheryl turns around to start typing on the container's keyboard.

"They are looking for something, looking so bad that they started killing the crew and trainees."

Robert pulls the dead pirate's body into the container, while the container's front doors start closing,

"What are they looking for?"

Cheryl presses more keys to lock the container with the pirates inside it.

"A relic."

"A what?" asks Robert as he puts on the dead pirates' ammo vest.

"A Relic...Have no Idea...I just said that I knew where it was so that they'd stop the killing..."

Robert pulls Cheryl's head close to his, saying

"Your one gutsy girl you know! You really thought you could take on two pirates by yourself?"

Cheryl pulls back her head from Robert's hand

"Didn't know what I was thinking...Just trying to stay alive."

Robert then slams a fresh magazine clip into his rifle and says,

"So, what's next sweetheart?"

Cheryl starts walking and Robert follows her.

"The only reason why they're not in a hurry to leave is that they could be jamming our distress signal to the IC. We must get on their ship and disable it."

Robert grabs Cheryl's arm

"Wait a minute! There's just the two of us! This isn't an Academy simulation kid. This is the real thing! Do you expect us to crawl around a pirate ship and disable their jamming device? You're crazy!"

Cheryl pulls back her arm and continues walking...

"Think about it Robert, you're a pirate, flying through unrestricted space, making sure your ship isn't being detected by the IC. God knows for how long that crew has been out of that piece of junk! I've seen their crew. They're like kids in a candy store. You think they'd want to miss out going on board a large vessel like ours?"

Robert slowly answers "No..."

Cheryl then walks to the next corridor airlock and says...

"Let's go then. I know what level they entered the ship. We're going to need some space suits before going to the pirate ship."

Cheryl and Robert start making their way to the level where the pirate ship is connected to the Titan by the umbilical link.

They go through a corridor where different small labs are used to check mineral samplings.

Robert peeks through the corner of the plexiglass window to check if the lab is clear. He sees two pirates in the lab making fun of an elderly man tied to a chair. He notices their weapons are on another table, a good distance from the pirates.

Robert hand signs to Cheryl, they rush to the lab and catch the two pirates by surprise. Robert shouts

"Down on the ground! Hands behind your heads!"

The pirates, surprised and without saying a word, comply. As Robert pointed his rifle at the pirates, Cheryl goes to the elderly lab man and cuts him free from his chair. Robert tells the two pirates to move to a smaller containment room in the lab and take off their space suits.

The elderly man says to Cheryl

"Thank God you both came. I thought they had killed everyone on the ship."

Cheryl, while trying to dress the old man's wounds says

"They're pirates, they want to keep some crew for ramson sometimes."

The old man answers

"Not an old man like me. I'm worthless."

While Cheryl finishes bandaging the old man, she says

"They are looking for some relic or something..."

The old man suddenly grabs Cheryl by the arm and says,

"The relic!"

"Do you know anything about it?" Cheryl asks. The elderly man takes a deep breath and slowly closes his eyes momentarily

"I was wondering when someone would be coming for that..."

"That? Do you mean the Relic? You know something about it?"

The old man stands up and heads for his personal workstation. He types in his security code and opens his monitor showing Cheryl his personal log from twenty-five years ago.

"I was part of an expeditionary team that went to Kepler-62f. A cold planet. It started as a regular survey. But as we were getting closer, we picked up a beacon that could have only been made by intelligent life.

The beacon led us to an ancient alien craft in orbit of the planet. When we finally figured out how to enter the ship, we did not find any lifeform, it almost seemed that the craft was abandoned by its occupants.

The interior of the ship was made of an unknown metal, silver metallic in color, almost as smooth as chrome. I entered what seemed to be the control room of the craft.

The outlay of the instruments and the interior of the craft seemed to be fit for a humanoid life form.

There was what seemed to be a central control area, something that would logically be a captain or Pilot's chair. I tried sitting on it, then a few seconds later, vibrating sounds and lights came on.

The ship's interior started shifting outwards and the walls were starting to illuminate and come alive.

My companions panicked and started dashing out of the craft. Then suddenly, a gold flat disk floated out of the alien instruments in front of me. It was circular and thin, had 4 holes that went through it, and it was about the size of my hand.

I could hear the rest of the crew in my helmet comms panicking and shouting for me to get out of the craft.

But something somehow has taken my mind off the panicking crew. I reached out my hand to grab the disk, and a bright flashing light overwhelmed me. A light that did not hurt my eyes, as if it were my mind seeing the light rather than my eyes.

All other sounds were drowned out by an increasing sound of silence. I felt my body floating. It felt, how should I describe it...almost spiritual.

I suddenly started seeing the stars and the planets go by me as if I were a comet hurling across the universe. The sense of time escaped me and I could not remember how long I was traveling through space.

The next thing I knew, I was lying in a hospital bed with health sensors around my head and body.

A woman came to my bedside wearing a hazard-protective outfit, which covered her whole body except her deep green eyes. She hovered over me. She had smiling eyes. She said they found me in the middle of a public garden."

Cheryl looks back at the old man

"They found you in a garden?"

The old man chuckles

"Yeah, space suit and all! They actually thought I fell out of the sky from a crashing craft."

Cheryl, with a confused face

"So what's so funny about that?"

The old man glances at Robert and turns back to Cheryl

"Oh, nothing is Funny about it, until I tell you they found me on Earth. I have never been to Earth, but always dreamed of going there someday, and I finally did!"

Robert started bringing the black pirate suits to the room and says

"Sorry to interrupt this universal spiritual journey but we have a job to do!"

Robert reminded. The old man stands up holding his injured arm and says

"Everyone thinks it's bullshit, even if they cannot explain how I got to earth on the same star date as our mission to Kepler-62f."

Cheryl and Robert start putting on the pirate's black space suits when Robert says

"So old timer, what happened to the relic?"

The old man started walking, staggering to a large crew locker cabinet, taking out a rusty metal box, hands it to Cheryl.

"They made a report to suit their claim as a Hallucinatory Event, even if my records and the crew on Kepler 62f checked out. I Guess the bureaucracy on Earth thinks I'm a liability."

Cheryl slowly opens the rusty box, inside it, wrapped in a purple velvet pouch was the Relic.

"They ran tests on it. Other than not knowing what it is made of, they did not see any reason for a crazy old man like me not to have it."

The old man said. Robert double-checks the captive pirates' restraints and places thick duct tape over their mouths.

"That should keep them quiet for a while."

Cheryl places the relic back into the velvet pouch and slips the relic into her breast pocket. Cheryl says,

"Thank you..." She stammers, not knowing the old man's name.

"George!" you can call me George."

"Thank you, George, we could use this as bait to get those scumbags off the Titan," Cheryl says.

Robert interrupts

"Time to Go! George, Go to the sublevels near the fusion reactors. I have cleared that area."

"I will, young man. Please be careful."

Cheryl, fixing her glove says,

"If I can, I will return it to you."

George Gives them a smile and says,

"I'm sure you'll do your best."

Robert and Cheryl started their way to the mechanical umbilical that connects to the pirate ship. Robert takes a look down the other end of the umbilical

"There are two guards on the other end. Both not wearing their space helmets. Remember, there is no gravity in there, so your weapons fire will push you in the opposite direction...helmets on."

He grabs an empty bottle of wine left by other pirates in the corridor.

"What's that for?" Cheryl asks.

"Props! Pirates always carry stuff to their vessel."

Robert floats into the tunnel-like structure and Cheryl follows. Roberts starts mumbling, slurring loudly, acting like a typical drunk pirate while the two pirates guarding the other end take one look at them and then continue their own conversation.

Robert continued floating and mumbling drunkenly as they got closer to the two guards. Cheryl floating behind casually slips her hand to her sidearm. When Robert got close enough to the first guard, he asks

"Aren't you guys coming over for a drink?"

The pirate guard stared at Robert's helmet, trying to make out who he was. Cheryl was watching the guard's facial expression.

The second guard started noticing Cheryl's bright orange-red uniform under the black space suit at the neck area. The guard started to reach for his rifle, but Cheryl fires her sidearm twice, forgetting to anchor herself, she began tumbling back down the weightless corridor. Her bullets hit the pirate.

Robert grabs the other pirate by his space suit collar opening and thrusts his helmet forward to smash down on the pirate's face.

While Cheryl is trying to stop herself from floating back towards the Titan, another pirate comes into the tunnel from the Titan. The Pirate Sees what is going on and lets go of the crates and boxes he was carrying to reach for his rifle.

Cheryl, while trying to grab the walls of the tunnel, loses her sidearm. Robert grabs his sidearm and puts two bullets into the pirate, still holding on to the pirate's neck ring.

He turns around to see the third pirate from the Titan grabbing his rifle and starting to point it at Cheryl.

Cheryl was struggling to get to her rifle slung behind her while floating uncontrollably.

Robert quickly placed his back against the wall at the end of the umbilical wall to secure himself. He took careful aim with his rifle.

The Pirate started shooting at Cheryl, but by some miracle, the crates the pirate let go of were blocking the aim of the pirate.

The pirate started hitting the crates spinning in the weightless corridor, bouncing off the walls, and splintering into several floating pieces. Robert could feel some of the bullets going into the wall just inches from him.

Cheryl shouts "Robert!" A bullet graces off her left arm and she could see her blood, dark red droplets floating around her. Cheryl could see that the pirate had now a clear shot. She could see the barrel of the rifle pointed straight at her, she took one deep breath and closed her eyes, thinking it would be her last. Robert had hit the pirate with a headshot, flipping the body over in the gravity-less chamber.

Cheryl opened her eyes and saw the lifeless body of the pirate that she thought would end her life. She began to feel the sting of her bullet wound.

"Shit! I never got hit before..."

Then Robert says from the distance

"Scars are sexy, but we have to go! Now!"

Cheryl grabs her sidearm, pushes, and floats herself toward Robert.

"Are you ok?" Robert looks at Cheryl's Arm wound.

"Yeah, I'll live, just patch me up a bit." Robert sticks his head to peek into the entrance of the pirate ship

"Clear!"

He closes the access door to the umbilical and then pulls out a small canister of first aid spray from his chest pocket.

"Is that company-issued, or pirate issued?" asks Cheryl

"Does it matter? It will stop the bleeding..."

Robert starts spreading the hole opening of Cheryl's suit till he finds her wound.

He starts spraying, and a foamy white surface forms on Cheryl's wound.

"Feels Cold..." Cheryl says.

"Then we know it's working,"

says Robert as he opens another vest pocket to get an emergency suit patch.

"This should temporarily keep your suit working till we find another one. In the meantime, don't go wandering out to space..."

They pass several corridors looking for a way to the ship's bridge. Cheryl notices a ship map on the wall and starts tracing her fingers across it looking for its location.

"It should be two levels up this way..."

Eventually, they reach the bridge of the pirate ship. Robert secured the door while Cheryl immediately went for the communication panel. With swift keystrokes, she disables the pirate ship's jamming program that kept the Titan 3 from sending a distress call to the IC.

"That should do it! I'm sending another distress signal right now..."

Cheryl takes a quick look at her watch and says,

"They should be here in ... 5 hours."

Robert, looking at the different monitors showing the different parts of the pirate ship and says

"That's a long time. How do we keep the pirates from killing more of the Titan's crew in the meantime?"

Cheryl starts looking at the other comm controls in front of her.

"I could send a public address message to that blue-haired bastard keeping our captain, that we have the relic...Even showing it to him on Screen."

"There is another airlock that leads outside this ship, right there."

Robert points to one of the monitors showing an airlock.

"If we could get to it, we could get into another entrance to the Titan at the cargo level."

Cheryl says "A spacewalk? In these pirates' space suits? We're not familiar with its systems..."

Robert takes a quick glance at his suit and grabs his helmet.

"What's there to know? You wear one suit; you wear them all!"

The pirate captain was still in the bar, drunk like the other pirates, hollering and shouting while forcing the female crew captives to dance on stage.

Some of the pirates started throwing glasses and bottles around the lounge to show their dissatisfaction with the Crew's stage dancing.

The golden-haired scarred pirate was still sitting in the bar when one of the other drunk pirates came up behind her.

"C'mon Nova! Show these girls how to give a man a good time…"

She scornfully gazed at the pirate and said,

"I would rather kiss a Valerian Cobra than spend a minute with you."

The drunk pirate grabbed Nova by the thigh and started pulling her off her bar stool.

"You don't talk to me like that you bitch!"

Nova Swung her elbow straight at the pirate's nose breaking it. She followed it up with a beer bottle to his head that made him fall to the ground.

She stood up and put one boot across his neck, pulling out her sidearm, and pointing it down towards the pirate's face. Suddenly the whole room was silent except for the continuing music, as they all saw what Nova had done to the persistent pirate.

"Enough of this Nova! You don't have to kill him to make your point!"

Shouted the blue-haired pirate captain. Nova took her finger off the trigger and holstered her weapon saying

"Try that again, next time you won't have the captain to save your rotten life!"

She spits at the pirate's bloodied face as two other pirates grabbed him off the floor. She turns back to her stool, grabs a napkin on the bar, and starts wiping spilled beer off her scarred face and shoulders.

She looks at the mirror across the bar behind the bottles to check if her lipstick was ruined. Suddenly, the music stopped, and the image of Cheryl came on all the monitors and speakers on the Titan.

"To the pirate captain and crew on board the Titan 3, we have the relic that you are looking for. We are now in command of your vessel. We have disabled your jamming frequency and the Interplanetary Command will be here shortly.

Release all Titan 3 crew members and we will allow you to board your ship giving you a chance to peacefully leave before the IC comes into orbit. We shall leave the relic on your captain's chair. Considering the damage and loss of life due to your attack on the Titan, this is an exceptionally good offer. Resist and we will self-destruct your ship. You have 5 minutes to Respond."

The pirate captain stands up, finishes his glass of whisky in large gulps, then throws the whisky glass to the bar, smashing the mirror and causing several bottles on the shelves to fall. His officers quickly stand at attention.

"Call Barak and tell him to retake our ship! Go to all levels of the ship and tell our men to start heading back to the ship. Leave a few men to guard the captives and to look for that Cadet! I want her Alive!"

Back on the Pirate ship, Cheryl and Robert started sealing off the Corridor to the bridge.

"You think they'll go for it?" asks Robert.

"They'll have to. What's a pirate without a ship?"

Cheryl ties the purple velvet pouch on the pirate captain's seat armrest, grabs her rifle and helmet, and follows Robert down a narrow tube that leads to the airlock on the stern of the ship. The airlock had several thruster packs hanging on the airlock walls that easily attach to their space suits.

"Never seen so many thruster packs in a single airlock before..."

"That's because pirates usually attack ships with individuals spacewalking to their targets, just the way we are headed back to the Titan."

They both attach a tether to each other, clamped thrusters to their suits, opened the airlocks, and proceeded to the exterior of the pirate ship.

As they floated on just above the surface of the pirate ship Robert noticed the exterior gun turrets.

"Wait, we need a little more insurance before we head back to the Titan."

Robert adjusts his position by grabbing the surface of the ship, then uses his thrusters to head towards the ship's main guns. Cheryl does the same and follows Robert. When they get to the Ship's guns, Cheryl says

"You know what you're doing?"

Robert puts both hands on the large barrel and places his feet on the gun's base.

"As soon as I twist the barrel, grab the wires that are just below the base," he tells Cheryl.

Robert starts pulling on the barrel exposing small wires at the gun's base socket. Cheryl quickly grabs about 5 wires that are exposed.

"Yank them out hard!" says Robert.

"Cheryl started grunting while pulling off the wires. Suddenly sparks flew where the wires were severed.

"That will do it!" said Robert. "Three More to go"

They float to the rest of the pirate's vessels' main guns to disable them. When they got to the last turret, they could see the movement of the pirates through the small windows of the connective umbilical tunnel.

"it's just a matter of time before the pirates reach the bridge!"

Cheryl says. Robert then reaches for his thigh pocket and grabs an adjustable metal wrench. He adjusted the head wrench while sticking it inside the last gun barrel. When it was tight enough, he punches the wrench deeper down the gun barrel.

"That should do the trick!"

They both floated their way just above the umbilical tube where there were no windows for them to be seen by the pirates. They could see flashes of light from inside the umbilical telling them that the pirates have already begun to torch their way back to the pirate ship.

They slowly scale the surface of the Titan floating toward the lower cargo deck.

"There! You see it?" As Robert points to an external access not far from the main cargo entrance of the Titan.

They both float towards the entrance as Cheryl is amazed at the view of the bluish-green planet below them.

Robert notices Cheryl's amazement at the views of the large planet below them.

"Beautiful, isn't it? It's really different when you do spacewalks above planets. You really don't feel the vastness of the planet sitting on the bridge and looking through monitors, yet here we are, just being parasites, taking resources from other planets."

They reach the external access, then Robert starts punching in an emergency entry code. The Door slides open and Air rushes out of the small air containment area. They both enter and reseal the external door. It only took a few seconds for the chamber to equalize with air. A green light flashes and the interior door opens to the Titan.

Both, with their rifles, pointed forward, move slowly into the cargo compartment. Robert, with his eyes, fixed on the rifle sights slowly walks through the large containers, checking each long corridor for Pirates.

He sees two pirates standing guard at the entrance of one large container. He looks at Cheryl and points toward the guards. He then puts two fingers up at his eyes and signals Cheryl to go towards the next corridor to get a better shot. Cheryl complies and starts heading for the next corridor. Whispering through his communicator he says,

"You in Position?"

Cheryl answers "Copy. I've got the one on the left..."

Robert answers "Copy that...In Three, Two, One..." Both Pirates fall to the ground.

"Cheryl, go to the container, there must be some Titan crew members in there. I'll just make a wider circle around the cargo bay to make sure there are no other pirates here."

Cheryl answers "Copy that."

Cheryl opens the container and sees five security officers inside. She starts cutting their restraints and asks them

"Any more of you guys around here?"

An older security officer answers

"Just us. They executed the rest of my men…They didn't even ask us anything. Just started killing for sport!"

Robert comes back and says

"This area is clear. Before we head out, we need to coordinate our plan of attack to take back this ship. We already sent in for IC support. They will be here in a few hours."

One of the younger security officers said

"I saw some of the crew members brought to the science labs, while the others were sent to the rec areas."

Robert looked at the older security officer and said

"You guys up for taking the labs while we go for the rec area?"

The older security officer, with a stern hardened look on his face, grabbed one of the dead pirates' rifles and tossed it to one of his men.

"Miller! Go with Officer Thompson and Robert to the rec area."

He then took the second rifle and checked its magazine. He chambers a bullet in the rifle and yells

"C'mon, men! It's payback Time!"

Robert and Cheryl start taking off their pirate space suits, so they do not get hit by friendly fire, now that they had a few security officers on their side.

Security officer Miller takes the point while making their way to the rec area. Cheryl notices that the once noisy and pirate-filled corridors on the rec level were now quiet, with the occasional buzzing of damaged consoles, flickering lights, vandalized walls and furniture, and the soft sound of relaxing piped-in music that was still playing.

They slowly make their way back to the bar where she had last seen her captain and her co-trainees.

They crouch low below the level of the bar furniture to keep themselves out of sight. As they get closer to the stage, they see three pirate guards.

One, sitting close to the Titans Captain, still restrained, and passed out, while two of the pirates were making fun of first officer Akita tied to her chair.

The bodies of the Navigation officer and the cadet trainee were placed at the edge of the stage. Miller, not taking his sights out of his rifle toward the pirates, whispers...

"Do we take them out now?"

Cheryl answers

"We need more information...Let's try to take them alive."

Miller, not liking Cheryl's answer, frowns and says

"Ok, But no promises."

Robert positions himself in between Cheryl and Miller and says

"Miller, go towards the left of the stage. Let's spread out and surprise them."

Miller nods and starts low walking towards the left. Cheryle moves forward in the center while Robert starts moving toward the right side of the bar.

Miller, while trying to get a clear aim at one of the pirates toying around with officer Akita, accidentally pushes a table with his elbow and knocks an empty bottle off the table, making a loud crashing sound on the floor.

The pirates turn around and the pirate closest to the captain stood up and went for his rifle while the other two pirates start moving for their sidearms.

Robert stands up and yells "Stop!"

The pirate going for his rifle freezes while another continues to go for his sidearm. Miller fires at the pirate going for his sidearm and hits him.

The third pirate ran and reached for his rifle at the base of the stage. Cheryl fires at the pirate now hiding behind the furniture just in front of the stage. She misses but continues to fire. The artificial wood on the stage and furniture started splintering with the shots from Cheryl's rifle.

Miller's training starts kicking in as he maneuvers further sideways while Cheryl gives him cover fire. The pirate still frozen at the sight of Robert's rifle stares at him and slowly inches his way toward his rifle.

"Don't do it!" yells Robert.

While Cheryl and the other pirate were in a fierce gun battle, Miller had finally positioned himself for a clear shot. Miller fires two shots, the first one hitting the pirate's right side, then a second fatal headshot.

Robert, Miller, and Cheryl start moving forward, all now aiming their weapons at the remaining standing pirate. The pirate takes a quick look at his two fallen comrades and lifts both hands in surrender.

Robert grabs the pirate's rifle leaning on the side of a chair and says

"On the ground! Now!"

The pirate complies and gets on his belly. Miller comes in and puts a knee on the pirate's back while he violently restrains the pirate's hands behind his back.

"Where is your captain?" asks Cheryl.

"He went back to our ship..."

Miller hits the bounded pirate on his backside

"Where's the rest of your crew?! Where's the rest of The Titan Crew?!"

Cheryl checks on the Titan's Captain while Robert goes to First Officer Akita.

"Sir, you all right sir?" Cheryl asks while cutting the captain's restraints to the chair.

"I'm all right. Glad you made it back Thompson..."

Robert Frees Akita and hands her one of the pirate's rifles.

Akita Stands up, wipes her tears from her face, and walks towards one of the shot pirates whom Miller first hit, but was still alive. Akita started kicking the pirate's face and body.

Robert grabbed officer Akita by her right arm to stop her but was able to fire one shot at the pirate's face. Cheryl was just imagining what this pirate did to officer Akita to make her go wild like this.

The pirate's blood has splattered on Miller's face, who was checking another pirate's ammo belt. Cheryl, with her palms towards Akita, slowly walks towards her who was still pointing her rifle at the dead pirate

"It's all right now..., It's over."

The captain, now standing behind Akita slowly puts one hand on Akita's shoulder, and another hand slowly takes the rifle from her. The captain embraces Akita. Cheryl goes behind the Titan Captain and says

"Captain, we have our Security forces clearing the ship and they are on their way to Free the rest of the crew in the science labs level."

The captain slowly lets go of Akita as he sees she has begun to get hold of herself.

"We have to detach from their umbilical to get free of their ship. We must get to the bridge and seal off the corridor where they made a breach, and pull away from their ship."

Miller secures the tied-up pirate to a bar post, then they all head up to the Titans bridge.

The Captain takes his chair as First Officer Akita sits at her station.

"Engage engine start-up sequence."

Says the captain as both the captain and the first officer start activating each of their controls.

The bridge Lights up as the monitors and switches come alive.

"Starting sequence suspended due to offline reactor Captain." Says Akita.

"Try Emergency Bridge Command Override..." says the captain.

Akita switches her monitors and slides her screen to Override Command. She puts in the override sequence and the screen turns red and starts flashing override failure.

"Override commands not responding captain. Manual reset required!"

Robert asks the captain "What's wrong?"

The captain still looking at his forward controls says

"Someone has to manually reset the fusion controls so we could restart the Titans Engines..."

Robert says "I'll go! I know that area. Cheryl, stay here."

Cheryl turns to Robert

"The hell I will! I'm coming with you! Miller will make a better backup for security in case those bastards try to take the bridge again."

The captain gives a frustrated look at Robert and says

"I suggest you take Cadet Thompson's request. Better yet, I will make it easier for you. That's an order!"

Robert and Cheryl start making their way to the main power compartment of the ship. They enter the narrow catwalks where the main fusion reactor of the ship is located.

"The reactor reset control panel is on the lower level," Robert says.

Cheryl looks below to see the catwalk they are on, which leads to a spiraling staircase that goes around the main reactor, with many cooling pipes crisscrossing the main silo on every level.

"That s a long way down..." She says softly.

As they start heading down the staircase hugging the wall of the giant silo, they heard heavy echoing steps and a shouting voice from above.

"There they are!"

They look up and see three pirates with their rifles drawn and pointing at them. The pirates start firing as their bullets start bouncing off the walls of the silo and the pressed metal sheets at their feet.

The thunderous sound of the rifle fire vibrates the ice crusting on the cooling pipes and starts falling down the silo like fine snow.

Robert notices that if they continue downwards, the pirates will have a clear shot because there are no cooling pipes above the next area they are supposed to proceed to.

He then sees a door about 15 meters from where they were covered by the cooling pipes above.

"We have to make it to that door! It's the only way. We go further down; we'll be like sitting ducks!"

Cheryl fires a burst of rounds toward the pirates and looks at the door. She says,

"Cover me!"

Robert starts firing upwards as Cheryl runs for the door. As she punches in the keys to open the door, bullets barely miss her, bouncing off the metal door, walls and floor. Sparks fly off every bouncing bullet near her as she tries to finish entering her entry code.

The door locks open, but as she rushes in, a huge pirate, the same pirate that tried to take advantage of scarred-faced Nova at the bar, with his bandaged nose bridge bone, grabs Cheryl's rifle and tosses her across the room like a rag doll. She tumbles and hits the walls, almost knocking her out.

He picks up Cheryl and put her on his shoulder like a hunter carrying his prey. He carries her into one of the engineer's quarters and slams her on the bed. Cheryl, still dazed, tries to reach for her sidearm, but the huge pirate grabs her pistol and throws it aside while pinning her to the bed with his large body.

He starts trying to rip off Cheryl's uniform. In the struggle, her left chest pocket opens and out slips the relic. Cheryl tries to fight back only to be punched in the stomach by the burly pirate.

"I've never had fresh Cadet meat before..."

The pirate says while his sweaty face started dripping on Cheryl's exposed underwear. Cheryl struggles as the pirate has his huge hand holding both her arms pinned behind her with his weight. Cheryl closes her eyes as she begins to feel helpless while the pirate starts reaching down on her. Suddenly a loud shot rang out in the small room.

The pirate fell lifeless on Cheryl, as part of his skull, was torn out, splashing blood and brain matter all over the bed and Cheryl's face.

Cheryl pushes the dead pirate's body off her to see the gold-haired, scarred Nova holding a rifle with smoke slowly passing through the barrel.

Nova reaches for a dirty towel just hanging from the door of an opened metal locker and tosses it to Cheryl.

"I've been waiting a long time to blow that bastard's brains out!"

Nova says casually as she hangs her rifle on her shoulder and bends down to get Cheryl's sidearm. Cheryl starts wiping the pirates' blood off her face and starts pulling together her partially torn uniform.

Nova slowly hands Cheryl's pistol to her saying

"I'm Nova...here, you'll be needing this."

Cheryl confused asks "Aren't you one of them?"

Nova grabs the relic just beside Cheryl, who did not even realize it had come off her chest pocket in the struggle.

Nova holds it up to Cheryl's face and says,

"Where is the man you took this from?"

Cheryl, not being sure of the pirate woman's intentions answers

"What man?"

Nova takes a closer look at the relic bringing it closer to the wall light in the room.

"It's just the way I remembered it." Says, Nova.

"Five Years and not a scratch on it..."

Cheryl Stands up and heads to a small sink to wash her face. Nova turns to Cheryl and says

"So, is George still alive?"

Cheryl was surprised that Nova knew George's name, pausing as she was washing the pirate's blood off her neck.

"Who is George to you?" Asks Cheryl.

Suddenly, They could hear Robert running down the corridor outside the room shouting Cheryl's name. Robert comes through the door and sees Nova standing in the middle of the room holding the Relic up to the light. Cheryl shouts

"Don't shoot! She saved me!"

Nova takes a step back to show Robert the body of the dead pirate on the bed. Robert looks at the body, then turns to Nova and says

"But you're a pirate, right?"

Nova Smiles at Robert

"I pretended to be one of them just to get me here. I'm looking for George."

Cheryl finishes washing the blood off herself and tells Nova,

"Well, I think we know where to find George."

Cheryl starts opening the other lockers in the room and grabs a red engineering jumpsuit and toss it to Nova.

"You better change out of that pirate outfit if you don't like to get hit by one of our men."

The Pirate Captain and his men finally break into their bridge on the pirate ship. His officers went to their stations and checked the condition of their ship.

The Pirate Captain notices the small purple velvet pouch hanging on his seat's armrest. He smiles, but before he could open it, one of his officers interrupted;

"Captain! Titan security forces have regained control of their ship and are now at the umbilical."

The pirate captain strokes his jewel-laden fingers on his blue mohawk hair and starts punching at the controls on the right side of his seat.

"Tell the men to seal the outer doors!"

Another pirate officer yells

"But sir, we still have men on the Titan..."

The blue-haired pirate captain said

"We are pirates. Getting left behind is part of the job!"

The pirate captain swivels his head to another pirate at the controls and says "Prepare all guns for firing..."

Cheryl, Robert, and Nova make their way to the reset panel of the fusion reactor.

"We'll have to open this board to access the re-set switch. Tools, we need tools…"

Then a voice came out of the shadows between the large metal stacks of the fusion reactor…

"Tools you say! I have a lot of that."

They looked into shadows between the tall metal stacks to see the outline of a man carrying a large metal toolbox, who slowly came out of the shadows.

"George!" Robert says.

George's face comes out of the shadows staring at Nova.

"Nova! Is that you?"

Nova starts running towards George. He drops his toolbox, catching Nova as she gives him a tight hug with tears flowing down her eyes.

"I thought I'd never see you again, Nova,"

George says as he also starts sobbing with happiness.

"I found you, Papa. I found you!"

Nova continues sobbing like a twelve-year-old girl. Cheryl watches the father and daughter reunion, almost starting to tear up.

Robert nudges her and grabs the toolbox at George's feet.

"I guess the universe isn't big enough to keep a daughter from her father,"

Cheryl says as Robert opens the toolbox to bring out an electric screwdriver. As Robert and Cheryl start removing the panel, George and Nova sat down against the wall. George holds Nova's face and looks at her scarred face

"What have they done to you?" Asks George.

"I joined the pirates when I heard that their captain was after your relic. There were things I had to do to stay alive and convince them that I was one of them. I knew it would be the fastest way for me to find you."

George gently holds her daughter's face in his hands and says

"You really have your mother's green eyes. The same eyes that stared down at me when I found myself on Earth."

Robert finally removes the panel and exposes several wires and switches of different color codes.

"Which one do we reset?"

Asks Cheryl. Robert looks around and says

"The red one..."

George, upon hearing Robert and Cheryl's confusion walks to them while Nova follows.

"I've been here long enough to know that to reset the fusion reactor for the Bridge to gain control of it again, would be the fourth green switch from the left."

Robert spreads the wires apart to expose the hidden switches in the panel. He counts the switches from the left

"Two, Three. And...Four!"

He flips the switch, and a few seconds later, the whole reactor area started coming alive with humming sounds and vibrations, indicating the reactor has been reset.

Robert and Cheryl let out a deep breath of relief.

At the Titan's bridge, First Officer Akita is alerted by her instruments as they turn green.

"Captain, the fusion reactor is now online, and we have control..."

The captain makes a fist in the air and says,

"They Did it!"

The Titans captain takes off his gloves and rapidly opens and closes his hands making a tight fist before grabbing the flight sticks of his Ship in front of him.

He takes one serious look at First Officer Akita and says,

"The Captain now has control!"

Akita confirms with a smile.

As George gets back to Nova to continue their reunion, Robert and Cheryl get busy putting back the cover of the panel board.

The ship jerks violently from side to side.

"Looks like the captain got control again!" says Robert.

Cheryl bends down to put the electric screwdriver back in the metal toolbox. Shots rang out and started hitting the wall behind Cheryl. Robert quickly looked up and saw another pirate firing down at them.

Nova pulls her father behind steel pillars for cover and starts firing back at the pirate on the catwalk above them.

Cheryl stumbles on the metal toolbox and Robert quickly reacts by stepping in front of Cheryl, giving her time to get back on her feet.

Another shot rang out, and Robert was hit in the chest. Cheryl screams

"Robert! ...No!"

Nova Rushes to the left side position to get a clear shot at the pirate.

With three successive bursts, Nova finds her target, and the pirate fell off the catwalk to the bottom of the silo.

Cheryl rushes to Robert and pulls him to her lap. Blood was streaming out of his chest wound and Cheryl began applying pressure with both her hands.

"Where's the can?"

Cheryl, panicked, asked Robert while Nova and George saw that Robert's wound is a fatal one.

Robert Answers while trying to stay conscious.

"There's no more my love…"

Robert reaches for his thigh pocket and brings out his tiny remote-control device.

"Bring this to the bridge, and press the red-light button for three seconds… my one last favor…"

Cheryl says "No! we'll take you to the med bay. We'll fix you up!"

Robert smiles at Cheryl and says

"You were always a hardheaded woman. That's why I love you… See you later…"

Robert closes his eyes and he slowly stops breathing. Cheryl starts crying and holds Robert tightly with her blood-stained hands.

George and Nova slowly approach Cheryl

"We have to bring that device to the captain…" George says.

Cheryl opens her bloodied hand to see the tiny remote-control device that Robert gave her.

"Bring it to the bridge he said," says Cheryl.

"One last favor…"

At this point, the Titan's captain was busy maneuvering the titan up against the pirate ship. He was using the mechanical umbilical to whip the pirate ship against the large thick haul of the Titan.

The Pirate captain gives the order to fire, but his disabled guns fail to respond.

The pirate crew at the bridge says

"Captain, our lateral guns are not responding!"

The blue-haired captain gives out an angry growl and instructs his men to fire the main guns at the Titan. One of his crew members says

"Captain! We are too close to fire our main guns! We must first get some distance before..."

The Pirate captain pulls out his side arm and shoots his crew member before he could finish.

"Fire the main guns now!

Another pirate crew member pushes the dead body of his crewmate aside in order to take over his controls. He activates the main gun controls and the pirate's main guns online.

The main gun fired with the wrench lodged in its barrel, and the large gun exploded inwards, killing most of the pirates, and ripping a large portion of the pirate ship into space.

The Titan's captain tells the First Officer to instruct the security personnel to seal off the corridor that is attached to the Titan.

"Time to pull that damn thing off my ship!" the captain says angrily.

As First Officer Akita starts relaying the message to the crew. Cheryl, George, and Nova enter the bridge.

"Good work Officer Thompson!" The captain looks back and asks,

"Where is Officer Robert?" Cheryl stays silent as George answers "He did not make it captain, but he did have one last request."

The voice from the Security Officers goes on the speaker

"Sir, we have already sealed off corridor 14. You may now proceed with umbilical detachment..."

The captain looks at Cheryl and says

"Officer Thompson, you have permission to execute the last request."

Cheryl goes to First Officer Akita's station. Akita gives way and says

"Officer Thompson now has the comm."

At the Pirates bridge, the pirate captain opens up the purple velvet pouch and brings out Cheryl's lucky green stone. He screams in anger and starts bashing the instrument panels in front of him in frustration. His monitors then come alive with Officer Cheryl Thompson's face on the screen.

"I see that I have been outwitted by a Cadet Trainee! My Congratulations." the pirate captain says sarcastically.

"And I see you have found my lucky green stone..." Cheryl responds.

The pirate captain cuts her off by saying

"You think this is the end of this? There is no place in space where you can hide Officer Thompson! I will find you!"

Cheryl then cuts off the pirate captain saying

"Before you go, captain, I have another surprise for you...from Officer Robert Foster..."

She shows the tiny remote-control device.

The pirate captain's eyes widen and yells

"Give me Full speed Now!"

The Pirate ship tears itself away from the Titan, scattering the mechanical umbilical tumbling into space.

Cheryl presses the tiny red button for three seconds, and Robert's tiny mechanical droid climbs up from under the pirate captain's chair and deeply clamps into the pirate's forearm flesh. The same arm holding the lucky stone.

The pirate captain shouts in pain and his hand releases the lucky green stone that falls to the floor.

Then Cheryl says "This is CCS Titan 3.... Signing off."

The pirate's ship bridge explodes, cutting the forward section of the ship out of its main body. Cheryl watches as the Pirate ship tumbles out of orbit and starts its descent to the planet's atmosphere and to a fiery end below.

Three planet days passes and the IC had boarded the Titan 3. Repairs were being done and supplies were being shipped from the planet below.

Cheryl, dressed in a formal white uniform, and a golden officer's badge was standing alone over the casket of Robert that was draped in his colony flag.

She had been praying and being thankful for the time she had spent with Robert. She places her hand over the silver-grey-closed coffin. Her eyes shut. She started to remember all the good times they have spent together. Behind the coffin was a large window, with the stars and the planet below, slowly turning and reflecting its Sun's light on the thin layer atmosphere unto the Titans wide window.

The soft sound of the sliding door behind her activated and walked in George and Nova. George says in a soft voice.

"When you are ready, come to our quarters."

Both Nova and George gave Cheryl a light hug and left her once again to be alone in the room.

Later, Cheryl walked down the corridor to George and Nova's quarters. She presses on the door chime, but there was no answer. The sliding door opens and she entered slowly and started looking around.

"George...Nova..."

She went into the living room. There she saw a letter, and above it, hanging on a small table lamp was the relic. She opened the letter.

Dear Cheryl.

You must be wondering why we are not here. When I found the relic, the only thing on my mind at the time was being with my daughter, whom I haven't seen in years. She and her mother were transferred out of my colony during my deep space exploration assignment, and the last thing I heard of my family was that they were brought to Earth. My wife had contracted a deadly virus on earth. She died about a year before I found myself hurled to Earth by the Relic.

But the authorities did not believe my story. They thought I was crazy. So, they gave me a choice, stay on Earth in an asylum or take a lower-paying job as a material and mineral engineer. My daughter and I were separated, and her last words to me were that she would try to find me. You see, I could not use the relic if I wasn't sure where my daughter was.

I did not want to spend its powers jumping all over the galaxy looking for her.

So, I waited for her to find me. Now that we have found each other, we only have to use the relic just one more time, for us to be with my wife. You see, there are much more mysteries to the universe than what we perceive. The relic gives you the power to be in the reality you wish to be.

The key is to believe and have faith. Without belief and faith, it is just a piece of unknown metal with four holes around it.

By the time you are reading this letter, my daughter and I will be with my wife. Yes, my wife.

The relic will bring you to a dimension that goes beyond death, to worlds only your mind can imagine.

We will leave the Relic with you. Instructions on how to use it are attached to this letter.

Remember, you must have faith and believe.

May you find your journey through the universe together with the ones you love, a happy and everlasting one.

You deserve it.

Your Friend

George.

First Officer Akita enters the bridge.

"Sir, it's time for the Service."

The captain, also dressed in formal white takes his captain's hat off hanging on his chair, and says,

"Let's Go then."

The Officers marched and prepared to enter the chapel expecting Cheryl to be there, beside Robert's casket.

First officer Akita looks at the captain. Then the captain gives a nod signaling the First Officer to open the chapel's doors.

The door opens, and the room was empty. They looked at the casket where Roberts's body was, opened, and empty.

The captain sees the relic at the foot of the casket stand. He picks it up while the whole crew were all at a wonder of what has just happened.

"Akita!" The captain says while looking outside the large glass window. They both watch two bright comets, almost dancing, with their long bright tails sailing through the stars.

They both smile and the captain says,

"We are all really part of the stars."

The End